PUPPY PRIZES

LUCY DANIELS

Puppy Prizes

Illustrated by Paul Howard

Hodder
Children's
Books

a division of Hodder Headline Limited

Special thanks to Narinder Dhami

Text copyright © 2002 Working Partners Limited
Created by Working Partners Limited, London W6 0QT
Illustrations copyright © 2002 Paul Howard
Cover illustration by Chris Chapman

First published in Great Britain in 2002
by Hodder Children's Books

For more information about Animal Ark,
please contact www.animalark.co.uk

10 9 8 7 6 5 4 3 2 1

A Catalogue record for this book is available from
the British Library

ISBN 0 340 85206 2

Typeset by Avon Dataset Ltd, Bidford-on-Avon, Warks

Printed and bound in Great Britain by
The Guernsey Press Co. Ltd, Channel Isles

Hodder Children's Books
a division of Hodder Headline Limited
338 Euston Road
London NW1 3BH

Contents

1

The giant marrow

"Grandad!" Mandy Hope laughed as she put a gooseberry into her basket. "You're supposed to be *picking* the gooseberries, not eating them!"

Grandad winked at her. "Don't tell your gran," he smiled. He popped another plump, green berry into his mouth. "Mm, they're really juicy this year. Do you want one?"

Mandy shook her head. "No, thanks," she said. "They're too bitter. I only like them when they're cooked!" She stepped out of the row of gooseberry bushes and put her basket down on the grass. "Phew! I need a rest," she puffed. "Thanks for giving me these gloves to wear, Grandad. The bushes are *really* prickly!"

Mandy and Grandad Hope were in the garden at Lilac Cottage. The sun was blazing in a cloudless blue sky, and it was baking hot. It was the best weather Mandy could remember for ages, perfect for summer holidays.

"I hope it stays like this for the Seven Dales Dog Show," Mandy said, flopping on to the grass and pulling off her gloves. This year the show was being held in the village of Welford, where the Hopes lived. Mandy couldn't wait. She was counting down the days to the August Bank Holiday when the show would take place.

"Well, it's still a couple of weeks away," replied Grandad, putting down his basket beside her. "But it's been a lovely summer so far, so we might be lucky." He grinned at Mandy.

Mandy smiled back. Animals were her favourite thing in the whole world. Mandy's mum and dad were both vets, and their surgery was built on to the back of their house, not far from Lilac Cottage.

"Your dad's going to be the show vet, isn't he?" remarked Grandad, taking a red and white handkerchief out of his pocket and mopping his brow. "And your gran's getting ready for the show right now, cooking for the Women's Institute stall."

Mandy glanced over at the cottage. She could see her gran moving about in the kitchen, and delicious smells were drifting through the open window. "What's Gran making?" she asked.

Grandad Hope tapped his nose mysteriously. "Something very special, actually," he replied, his eyes twinkling. "She'll tell you all about it. Now, what time is James coming?"

"He should be here soon," Mandy said. James Hunter was her best friend. "He's really excited about measuring the marrow again!" She looked at the giant, dark-green marrow growing at the edge of the vegetable patch.

It was very long, and so thick that even Grandad couldn't wrap his hands all the way round it. Grandad was growing the marrow for the Harvest Festival in September. Mandy had been helping him to measure the marrow every few days and record the results in a notebook.

"I'm sure it's grown since the last time we measured it," Mandy said. "In fact, I can almost *see* it growing!"

Grandad Hope laughed. "Come on, love," he said, picking up his basket again. "Let's get these gooseberries picked, then we can have a cold drink."

Mandy put her gloves back on, and she and Grandad set to work again. Their baskets were getting quite heavy by the time Mandy's gran came out of the back door. She was carrying a tray with two tall glasses on it.

"I think you've done enough for today," Grandma Hope smiled, raising her eyebrows at the sight of the loaded baskets. "Come and have a drink."

Mandy carefully set her basket on the grass and picked up one of the glasses. "Thanks, Gran," she said, taking a sip of the clear liquid.

It looked like lemonade but it wasn't, even though it tasted cool and sweet and a bit lemony.

"Do you like it, Mandy?" asked Grandma Hope.

Mandy nodded and took another sip. "What is it?"

"Elderflower cordial," her gran replied, handing the other glass to Grandad. "I put some sparkling mineral water in too, just to dilute it a bit. It's got quite a strong taste."

Mandy's eyes widened. *"Elderflower*

cordial?" she repeated, staring at the big elder tree which grew near Grandad's compost heap. Its long, spreading branches were weighed down with large, cream-coloured flowerheads. "You mean, it's made from *those*?" she asked, pointing at the flowers.

"Yes, that's right," Gran said with a smile.

"How did you make it?" Mandy asked curiously.

"Well, I had to soak the elderflowers in boiling water with sugar and a lemon, then leave it for five days," her gran replied. "I've made a whole batch for the dog show."

Mandy grinned. "So *that's* what Grandad meant when he said you were making something special."

Grandma Hope nodded. "The WI members have decided to use things from our gardens and the countryside to make all the food and drink for our stall," she explained. "We're going to call the stall *A Taste of Olde England*."

"That sounds great!" Mandy said enthusiastically. "Are you going to dress up in old-fashioned costumes, too?"

Her gran laughed. "It might be a bit hot, in

this weather! Why don't you come and see what else I've been making?"

"OK," Mandy said eagerly. She followed her into the cottage, while Grandad brought the baskets of gooseberries.

The kitchen table was laden with all sorts of goodies. There were pots of different coloured jams, bottles of elderflower cordial and a cooling rack covered with rows of pale brown tarts.

"That's quince jelly," said Grandma Hope, pointing at the jam. "My friend Mary gave me some quinces from the tree in her garden."

"What are quinces?" asked Mandy.

"They're large fruits, shaped a bit like a pear," her gran explained. "We don't eat them much nowadays. Here, try one of these." She pointed to the rack of tarts.

Mandy took one and bit into it. The cake was soft and flaky, with a rich almond taste. "Mm! It's scrumptious!" she said.

"They're called Maids of Honour," Gran told her. "It's a recipe from Tudor times, so it's nearly five hundred years old."

"Maybe I should try one too," said Grandad

with a grin. "Just to make sure they're as good as Mandy says!"

Right at that moment the doorbell rang.

"That'll be James," Mandy said, finishing off her cake.

"I'll get it," offered Grandad.

"Thank you for helping to pick the gooseberries, Mandy," said Gran, carrying one of the baskets over to the sink. "I'm going to use them to make some pies for the stall."

"Oh, yum," Mandy said, her eyes shining. "I'm looking forward to the dog show even more now!"

Gran laughed. "You might not like *everything* we're selling on our stall," she warned. "Mrs Hart is making nettle soup."

"Nettle soup!" Mandy exclaimed, pulling a face. "That doesn't sound very nice."

"Wait until you taste it," Gran told her, as Grandad Hope and James came into the kitchen. James's Labrador puppy, Blackie, was on his lead, scurrying along with his tail wagging frantically.

"Hi, Mrs Hope," James said breathlessly. "Hello, Mandy."

Blackie spotted Mandy immediately. He

leaped towards her, barking with excitement.

"Blackie!" James scolded. "Stop that!" He was red in the face and sounded out of breath, as if he'd been running.

"Are you OK, James?" Mandy asked, bending down to fuss the puppy.

"I'm fine," said James. "Blackie and I ran all the way because I wanted to show you this." He pushed up his glasses, which had slipped down his nose, and held out a rather crumpled leaflet.

Mandy stared at it. "Oh!" she exclaimed. "It's the schedule for the Seven Dales Dog Show."

"It came in the post this morning," James explained. "I'm going to enter Blackie in some of the classes. There's one for Handsomest Pup."

"That's a great idea," Mandy said. She looked down at James's puppy, who was sniffing around under the table. With his short, dark coat and big brown eyes, Blackie was certainly a handsome pup!

Mandy quickly read through the leaflet. "What other classes are there? Oh, look, James. There are classes for pedigree dogs like spaniels and poodles. And there's one for Best Sheepdog. I *love* sheepdogs!"

"We're going to enter another class as well," James began. But before he could say anything more, Mandy noticed that Blackie was standing up with his front paws against the table leg, trying to reach a plate of cakes.

"Blackie, stop that!" she laughed. "Those are for Gran's stall!"

"So what other classes are you entering Blackie in, James?" asked Grandad Hope.

James looked a bit sheepish. "Well," he mumbled in an embarrassed voice, "I thought we might try the Best Trained Puppy class."

Mandy couldn't help smiling. James was always trying to train Blackie, but his puppy didn't seem very keen to learn!

"I know Blackie's a bit naughty, but there's a few weeks to go before the show," James went on earnestly. "And it'll give us a chance to practise the stuff we've done before."

"Good idea," Mandy said. "I'll help you if you like."

"Great!" James said cheerfully.

"Now, what about this marrow?" Grandad picked up a tape measure from the dresser and waved it at them. "Mandy, could you bring the notebook?"

Everyone went outside to measure the enormous marrow. Gran held Blackie on his lead, while Grandad Hope and James crouched down in the vegetable patch with the tape measure. Mandy stood on the path with the notebook and pencil.

"It's sixty-three centimetres long," announced James, peering at the tape measure.

Mandy wrote it down and looked at the previous measurements. "Wow! It's grown

three centimetres since last time," she exclaimed.

"And it's forty-four centimetres round," James went on.

"That's another two centimetres," Grandad worked out. "And it's still growing!"

"I wonder how much bigger it'll get?" Mandy said.

"Maybe we should find out how big the biggest marrow in the world is?" suggested James.

Grandad Hope laughed. "I think it was well over a metre," he said. "So we've got a long way to go yet."

"Well, at least this marrow will be the biggest in Welford," James said with a grin. Then he frowned. "Blackie, stop that!" And he dashed over to stop his puppy chewing Grandad's petunias.

Mandy laughed. "I think we'd better start Blackie's training as soon as we can!" she joked.

2

The training begins

"James is entering Blackie in the Best Trained Puppy class?" Adam Hope lowered his newspaper and raised his eyebrows at Mandy. "Well, that *will* be interesting!"

Mandy couldn't help laughing at the look on her dad's face. "I think it's a great idea, Dad," she said, taking a bite of toast. It was the following morning, and the Hopes were having breakfast. "James really wants to do it."

"Yes, but does Blackie?" Mr Hope teased.

Mandy grinned. "I don't know, but we're going to find out!" she said. "James wants me to meet him and Blackie this morning on the village green for some training."

"I agree with you, Mandy. It's a very good idea." Emily Hope carried a pot of tea over to the kitchen table. "The class will be a great chance for James and Blackie to show what they've learned so far."

"And the rest of the show looks really exciting, too," Mandy added, finishing off her toast. "Have you seen the list of pedigree classes, Dad? There are going to be *loads* of different dogs there."

Adam Hope nodded. "The show's bigger than ever this year."

"We can walk to the green together this morning, Mandy," said her mum. "I have to go to the Post Office. Your dad's taking morning surgery on his own."

"And I ought to get a move on." Mr Hope drank his tea quickly and stood up. "Good luck with Blackie's training, Mandy." He grinned at her. "You're going to need it!"

★ ★ ★

After finishing their breakfast, Mandy and her mum set off through the village. It was still quite early, but it already felt warm and the sky was a clear blue, with puffy white clouds drifting lazily along.

"I think Blackie is loads better than he used to be, Mum," said Mandy as they walked past the church.

"Yes, he is," Emily Hope agreed with a smile. "But Blackie is also a very lively, energetic pup, and a few more lessons won't do him any harm."

"We're going to use lots of rewards so it will seem like fun to him," Mandy explained.

"There they are now." Her mum pointed at the village green ahead of them. In the distance Mandy could see James and Blackie walking across the grass. Blackie was bounding along playfully as usual, straining at the lead.

"Oh, that's another thing," Mrs Hope warned Mandy with a smile. "Blackie will have to learn to walk without pulling at his lead, or the judges won't be too impressed! Now, I must go and buy those stamps." She gave Mandy a kiss and set off towards the Post Office.

Mandy walked over to James and Blackie. James didn't notice her at first. He was too busy trying to make Blackie sit down. "Sit!" he said firmly, trying to push Blackie's bottom towards the ground. But the puppy had already spotted Mandy coming towards them. He shot off like an arrow and flung himself at Mandy's legs. She bent down to pat him.

"Hi, Mandy," called James.

Mandy hurried over to him, Blackie at her heels. "Hi! How's it going?" she asked.

"Well, I thought we'd start with getting Blackie to sit," James explained. "Because he *does* do it sometimes – when he feels like it!"

"That sounds like a good place to start, then," Mandy agreed.

James looked at the puppy, who was standing beside Mandy with his tail wagging. "Blackie, sit down!" he said loudly.

Blackie trotted over to James and began to tug at the laces on his shoes.

James groaned. "That isn't what he's supposed to do!"

"But you were saying 'sit' before," Mandy reminded him. "And now you're saying 'sit down'. Maybe Blackie doesn't realise what you mean."

"Oh, yes." James clapped a hand to his forehead. "Your dad told me ages ago that I always had to use the same words."

Mandy grinned. "Why don't you try again?"

"Blackie," called James, getting the pup's attention. "Sit!"

This time, to Mandy's delight, Blackie actually *did* sit, although he bounced up again after a second or two.

"Well done, Blackie!" James exclaimed. He went over to the puppy, who was sniffing around in the grass, and gave him a dog biscuit. Blackie wolfed it down, looking very pleased with himself.

Suddenly James shook his head and turned to Mandy. "I've done it wrong again, haven't I?" he said, pulling a face. "I should have given Blackie the biscuit while he was sitting, not when he stood up. Now he thinks I've given him a treat for sniffing the grass!" He turned round to see where the puppy had got to. "Oh, no! Blackie, come back!"

Blackie was racing off across the green. Mandy could see that his eyes were fixed on a large tabby cat sitting on a wall near the Post Office. "He's spotted a cat, James!" she gasped. "Quick!"

They chased after Blackie, and finally caught up with him on the edge of the green. The cat jumped gracefully down from the wall and disappeared, but Blackie carried on barking fiercely.

"Come here, you bad boy," scolded James, clipping the lead on to Blackie's collar.

"Maybe we'd better just practise walking

him up and down on the lead," Mandy suggested. "In case that cat comes back!"

"Hello, Mandy, hello, James," called a voice behind them.

Mandy turned to see Mrs Trigg from Holly Cottage waving as she walked toward them. At her heels trotted Holly, her pretty black terrier-cross puppy. Holly's tail began to wag as soon as she spotted Mandy, James and Blackie. But she stayed beside her owner, even though she wasn't on the lead.

"Sit, Holly," said Mrs Trigg, as Mandy and James went over to say hello.

Holly sat down obediently, tail still wagging.

"See, Blackie?" James said sternly. "*That's* how you should do it!"

Blackie wasn't taking any notice. He dragged James towards Holly and the two dogs sniffed at each other. Holly stayed sitting even when Mandy and James bent down to give her a pat.

"I'm glad I saw you," said Mrs Trigg, smiling at them. "I wanted to tell you that Max and Sandy are coming to stay with me for the rest of the holidays."

"Great!" Mandy said, looking at James in delight. They'd got to know Mrs Trigg's grandson, Max, and his Cairn terrier puppy, Sandy, when they'd stayed with Mrs Trigg one Christmas.

"They're looking forward to seeing you, too." Mrs Trigg took a small rubber ball out of her pocket and threw it across the grass. "Holly, fetch!"

At once, Holly leaped up and raced after the ball. She stopped it neatly with one paw and picked it up in her mouth. Blackie whined and pulled on his lead, but James kept a firm hold on him while Holly trotted back towards her owner.

"Good girl, Holly!" called Mrs Trigg.

Mandy watched admiringly as the puppy dropped the ball at Mrs Trigg's feet. Holly was *really* well-trained. Mandy had a sudden thought. "Mrs Trigg, are you entering Holly in any of the classes at the Seven Dales Dog Show?" she asked.

Mrs Trigg stroked Holly and shook her head. "No, I don't think so," she replied. "I'll be too busy helping with the WI stall."

"Oh, that's a shame," Mandy said. "I'm sure Holly would be great in the Best Trained Puppy class. She's so well-behaved."

"Yes, she's really obedient," added James.

Mrs Trigg looked very pleased. "Oh, do you think so?" she said. "I *have* spent quite a bit of time training her. But then, she picks things up very quickly. She's so clever."

Mandy smiled to herself at the proud look on Mrs Trigg's face. It was hard to believe that Mrs Trigg had once been someone who didn't like pets at all! That is, until she'd met Sandy and Holly.

"Max will be here while the dog show is on," Mrs Trigg went on. "And you know how much he loves dogs! I'm sure he'll be interested in entering some classes with Sandy."

"Brilliant," said Mandy, grinning at James. "Maybe we can train Sandy and Blackie together?"

"That would be great," James agreed.

Mandy felt even more excited about the show. It would be fantastic to enter both Blackie and Sandy in the Best Trained Puppy class. But it was a shame Mrs Trigg didn't have time to enter Holly too. Holly could give them all lessons in good behaviour!

3

Disaster in the garden

"Look, this is a good one." Mandy showed James the leaflet she was holding. It was four days later, and they were sitting on the living-room floor in Animal Ark, sorting through some leaflets that Mr Hope had given them. They were all about how to train dogs.

"This one says don't try to do too much at a time," said James, looking at another leaflet.

"And to give lots of praise when the dog is doing something right." He raised his eyebrows at Mandy. "That doesn't happen very often with Blackie!"

"He's very quiet right now," Mandy commented, turning round to see where the puppy had got to. Then she burst out laughing. Blackie was lying on the rug, chewing a leaflet called *How to Train Your Puppy*.

"Oh, Blackie!" groaned James. Then he caught Mandy's eye and began to laugh as well. He rescued the soggy leaflet and put it in the bin.

"Is it time to go to Lilac Cottage yet?" asked James as they gathered up the rest of the leaflets.

"Oh yes, I almost forgot." Mandy jumped to her feet. Gran and Grandad had invited them round to Lilac Cottage for tea, and to measure the marrow again. "We'd better go."

They went out into the hall, and James put Blackie's lead on while Mandy popped into the surgery. The last patient had just gone and her mum was writing up her notes.

"Mum, James and I are going round to Lilac

Cottage now," Mandy told her.

Mrs Hope glanced up from her notepad and smiled. "Fine. See you later."

As Mandy and James hurried towards the front door, the bell rang. Wondering who it could be, Mandy opened it.

"Max!" she exclaimed in delight. "And Sandy!"

Max stood on the doorstep, grinning at Mandy and James. Beside him stood his Cairn terrier, Sandy, wagging his tail and staring up at them with his bright eyes.

"Gran told you we were coming, didn't she?" said Max. "We thought we'd pop round and say hello."

"It's great to see you again!" Mandy beamed. She knelt down to give Sandy a proper welcome, and the puppy immediately stood up on his back legs and put his shaggy little paws on her knees.

"Hi, Max," said James. "I think Blackie's glad to see you too!"

Blackie seemed to recognise his old friends, and lunged forward to greet Sandy. The two puppies sniffed at each other in a friendly way.

"We're just on our way to Lilac Cottage to

have tea with Gran and Grandad," Mandy said to Max. "Why don't you and Sandy come with us?"

"Would that be all right?" Max asked.

"Of course," Mandy told him. "Gran and Grandad would love to see you and Sandy."

Max nodded. "OK then," he said happily. "That sounds like fun!"

They set off through Welford with the two dogs trotting beside them. Sandy stayed beside Max but Blackie was being quite boisterous, tugging James along the path as he tried to investigate all the different smells.

"Blackie!" James protested, trying to pull the puppy back to heel. "You're going to have to learn to walk properly before the dog show."

"Gran told me about the show," Max said excitedly. "She said you were going to enter Blackie in some classes."

James nodded. "Are you going to enter Sandy?"

"I thought *maybe* I could enter him in the Best Trained Puppy class," said Max. "He can already do things like 'sit' and 'stay'. And there's a Best Terrier class too."

"You'd do well in that, wouldn't you, boy?" Mandy said, running her hand over Sandy's thick, golden-coloured coat. She stopped when she felt something prickly in his fur. "Oh, what's this?"

It was a burr. There were quite a few stuck in Sandy's shaggy coat, and Mandy knelt down and combed her fingers through his fur to ease them out.

"Sandy kept running into the hedge on the way here," sighed Max. "It's very hard to keep him clean. His coat gets messy really quickly."

"That's because it's so long," Mandy said, getting to her feet.

"And it's curly, too," added Max. "I spend ages brushing it, and even then it won't lie flat!" He frowned. "I just hope I can keep him clean for the show."

"Shall we have a go at training Blackie and Sandy tomorrow?" James suggested, as they arrived at Lilac Cottage. "The village green's a good place."

"Great idea," Max said eagerly. "Are you going to come too, Mandy?"

"Try and stop me!" Mandy laughed.

She rang the bell, and Grandad Hope opened the door. He beamed when he saw Max and Sandy. "Hello, you two," he said, bending down to pat Sandy on the head. "It's lovely to see you. Come in. You'll stay for tea, won't you?"

"Thanks, that would be great," said Max.

"We could do with another hungry mouth," joked Grandad as he led the way down the hall to the kitchen. "You know Mandy's gran – there's always enough food to feed an army!"

"Where *is* Gran?" Mandy asked, looking round the empty kitchen.

"She just popped out for some milk," Grandad told her. "She won't be long."

"This looks great!" said James, his eyes lighting up as he stared at the kitchen table. There were plates of thick sandwiches and scones spread with jam, and a large Victoria sponge.

"Isn't there any nettle soup?" Mandy asked, pretending to be serious. She started to laugh when she saw that both James and Max were looking a bit alarmed.

"*Nettle* soup?" Max repeated.

Mandy explained about the WI stall at the dog show. Meanwhile, Sandy and Blackie sniffed eagerly round the table, looking very interested in all the delicious smells.

"I think we'd better take the dogs out into the garden," said Grandad. He opened the back door and looked out. The air was still very warm, but the sky was overcast and quite grey, and there wasn't even a gleam of sunshine. "It looks like we might have a storm tonight," he said. "A dose of rain will be good for my marrow."

"Can we measure it now, Grandad?" Mandy asked, as Blackie and Sandy raced off down the garden, nipping playfully at each other's heels.

Grandad nodded. "You'd better fetch the tape measure, Mandy."

Max looked amazed. "Why are you measuring a *marrow*?" he asked.

Mandy grinned. "James can tell you," she said, as she hurried back into the kitchen.

She found the tape measure and notebook neatly tidied away in one of the dresser drawers. When she went outside again, Grandad, James and Max were admiring the huge marrow at the bottom of the garden. Blackie and Sandy were chasing each other round Grandad's wheelbarrow, which stood on the path next to the marrow.

"Wow! It's huge!" Mandy could hear Max saying.

She walked across the lawn towards them, smiling at the sight of Blackie tearing round the wheelbarrow, trying to catch Sandy. Every so often the little Cairn terrier stopped and crouched down on his front legs, wagging his tail playfully at Blackie. But as soon as Blackie got near him, he darted away again, round the other side of the barrow.

Blackie was obviously getting a bit frustrated with this, because, as Mandy watched, he suddenly decided to take a short cut to get to Sandy. With a cheerful woof, he jumped up into the wheelbarrow, which began to rock from side to side.

"Blackie!" Mandy called. "No!"

Too late. As Blackie scrambled to the other side of the barrow, it toppled over. To Mandy's horror, the wheelbarrow crashed to the ground, landing right on top of Grandad's marrow!

4

Max's good idea

There was a loud squelching sound. Mandy
clapped a hand to her mouth, hardly able to
believe what had happened. Blackie had
jumped out of the wheelbarrow just before it
hit the ground, so he was safe. Now he stood
on the path, wagging his tail and looking very
pleased with himself. But what about the
marrow?

"*Blackie!*" James was pale with shock. "What have you done?"

"Sandy!" called Max, as white-faced as James. "Come here *now*."

Mandy could hardly bear to look at Grandad. He was staring down at the wheelbarrow as if he couldn't believe his eyes.

"I'm really sorry, Mr Hope," said James in a wobbly voice.

Grandad Hope rested a hand on James's shoulder. "It's all right, James," he said quietly. "Accidents will happen."

Mandy rushed over to them. "Let's lift the wheelbarrow up," she suggested, hoping against hope that the marrow would be all right. It didn't seem very likely, though. They'd all heard that awful squelching noise, and it was obvious that part of the marrow had been squashed.

Mandy held Blackie by the collar while James helped Grandad to lift the wheelbarrow. With all the serious faces around him, Blackie seemed to know that he'd done something wrong. He pressed his warm body close to Mandy, his ears drooping. For once, his tail stopped wagging.

Grandad wheeled the barrow away, and Mandy looked down in dismay at the ruined marrow. The wheelbarrow had smashed right into one end of it and she could see the pale, yellowy-green pulp inside. Mandy swallowed hard, feeling very upset. It was a terrible waste, after all Grandad's hard work.

"How's the marrow-measuring going?" Grandma Hope came out of the back door. "Dear me! What are you all looking so miserable about?"

"The wheelbarrow fell on Grandad's marrow," Mandy explained quietly.

Gran gasped and hurried over to look. "Oh, Tom!" she said, patting Grandad's arm. "How on earth did that happen?"

Grandad glanced at James, who was red with embarrassment. "There was a bit of an accident," he said. "It wasn't anybody's fault. Is it time for tea now?"

Gran nodded.

"First we'd better move the poor old marrow out of my vegetable patch," said Grandad Hope. "I think I'll put it in the shed for the moment, until I decide what I'm going to do with it. James, could you give me a hand?"

Mandy watched sadly as Grandad cut the marrow free from the plant. Then he and James picked it up. James grunted with the effort – it really had been a monster marrow, thought Mandy. They carried it solemnly into the shed where they rested it on one of Grandad's seed tables. Grandad had to wrap the squashed end in a black plastic binbag, to stop the pieces falling everywhere.

"I don't think I'm very hungry," James whispered gloomily to Mandy as they went inside to have tea.

Mandy didn't feel like eating either. What an awful thing to have happened. Grandad wouldn't be able to take his giant marrow to the Harvest Festival after all . . .

"I still feel really bad," James said to Mandy as they walked through Welford the following morning. They were going to Holly Cottage to meet Max and Sandy so that they could practise for the show. "Your grandad was so nice about it, too."

"He didn't blame you, James," Mandy assured him. "Poor Blackie didn't mean to knock the wheelbarrow over." She bent down to pat the Labrador puppy, who, for once, was trotting along quietly on his lead. "And Gran's tea was delicious, wasn't it?"

James nodded, looking more cheerful. "I'm glad we didn't waste it!" he said.

Mandy smiled. Although everyone had been gloomy to begin with, they'd all felt a bit better after tucking into some tasty sandwiches and scones.

"I'm going to try really hard to train Blackie from now on," James said in a determined voice. "If he behaves a bit better, maybe he won't have so many accidents."

Mandy opened the gate of Holly Cottage. "Well, he seems to be behaving himself this morning," she pointed out, as Blackie stayed glued to James's heels. Then she laughed as Blackie jumped sideways and snapped at a big bumble-bee that had buzzed too close to his nose.

Max opened the front door, and Sandy and Holly appeared beside him. "Hi, we're ready to go," he said. "I'll just tell Gran."

"Is that Mandy and James?" Mrs Trigg popped her head round the kitchen door. "Hello, you two. Excuse me if I don't come out, but I'm just in the middle of making some gingerbread for the dog show."

Max knelt down to put on Sandy's lead, and Holly gave a little bark, wagging her tail furiously.

Mandy patted the excited puppy on the head, feeling a bit sorry for her. Holly obviously thought she was coming too! "Not today, girl," she murmured, scratching Holly's ears.

"Mandy, would you like to take Holly with you?" called Mrs Trigg. "I haven't had time to give her a proper walk this morning."

"Yes, please!" Mandy said, delighted. Max handed her Holly's lead, and she clipped it on to the little dog's collar.

They set off for the village green. Holly seemed very happy to be taken out by Mandy, and her short fluffy tail never stopped wagging. Mandy had adored Holly ever since Sandy had found the little puppy alone and injured one snowy Christmas. And Holly seemed especially fond of her too.

"Blackie!" James said crossly. The puppy had started pulling on his lead again, instead of walking properly. "How am I going to

stop him doing that?" he asked Mandy and Max.

"You could teach him to heel," Max suggested.

James sighed. "But we're still working on 'sit'!"

"Sandy's quite good at sitting," Max said proudly. He let the Cairn terrier off the leash, and Sandy immediately began to scamper round Blackie and Holly, sniffing at them.

"Sandy!" called Max. "Come here."

Sandy ignored him and pretended to nip Blackie's ear.

Max turned pink. "He's not very good at coming when he's called," he admitted. "We'll have to practise that for the show." He raised his voice. "Sandy! Come here!"

This time Sandy trotted over and cocked his head to one side as he gazed up at his owner.

"Sit!" Max told him, and Sandy sat. "Good dog!" And Max bent down to make a big fuss of his puppy.

"Mandy, why don't you try that with Holly?" suggested James. "If Blackie sees the other dogs doing it, maybe he'll learn something!"

"OK," Mandy agreed, letting Holly off the lead. Holly stood still for a moment, sniffing the grass, then glanced up at Mandy as if to say *What do you want me to do?*

"Holly, sit," Mandy said firmly. She wondered if Holly would obey her, or if she'd only listen to Mrs Trigg.

Holly sat down on her bottom and lifted her head to look at Mandy.

"Good girl!" Mandy said, feeling thrilled. She knelt down and patted the puppy.

"Holly's really clever," said Max admiringly. "And I know Gran's spent ages training her."

"OK, Blackie, now it's your turn." James let Blackie loose, and the puppy immediately charged over to the other two dogs and began jumping around them. Max and Mandy called Sandy and Holly over and put them back on their leads, so that Blackie could concentrate.

Mandy watched as James gently pushed Blackie's haunches to the ground, saying *Sit*. After several tries, Blackie began to get the idea, especially as James fed him a dog treat every time he did it right.

"Now let's try it without me helping him,"

said James, walking a few paces away. He stared sternly at his dog. "Blackie, sit!"

At once Blackie ran over to James and jumped up at his legs, nosing eagerly towards the pocket with the dog treats in it. James groaned, but Mandy and Max couldn't help laughing.

"Blackie doesn't see why he has to sit down to get a dog treat," grinned Max. "He knows you've got them in your pocket!"

"Blackie, you're a really bad dog!" James scolded. He turned to the others. "This is hopeless."

"No, it isn't," Mandy told him. "You just have to keep trying."

"I think we've done enough for today," said James at last, as he tried yet again to make Blackie sit for longer than two seconds. They had been practising for most of the afternoon. "Let's come back tomorrow."

"OK," Mandy agreed. She called Holly to her and clipped on the lead.

"I can't wait for the dog show," said Max as they headed back to Holly Cottage. "It's going to be brilliant!"

Mandy nodded in agreement, but James didn't look quite so keen. "I'm not really looking forward to it any more," he said gloomily. "Blackie's not very good at his training, is he?"

"He'll get better," Max said encouragingly. "Sandy was hopeless at first, too."

"I know, but Blackie seems to forget everything I teach him!" James grumbled, stepping to one side to let a woman with lots of shopping bags get past them.

As the woman walked by, Holly strained forward to sniff curiously at the bags of food, pulling on her lead and dragging Mandy with her.

"Holly, heel!" Mandy said quickly.

Holly stopped pulling at once and stepped back to Mandy's side. Max and James looked very impressed.

"Well done," said James. "Blackie would have been inside that shopping bag before I could stop him!"

Mandy turned pink. "Well, it's easy getting Holly to behave," she said. "Mrs Trigg's trained her really well."

"Yes, but you're very good with Holly

too," Max pointed out. "That makes a difference."

"It's a shame Mrs Trigg's too busy to take part in the show with Holly," remarked James, opening the gate to Holly Cottage. "Holly's so good, she could easily win the Best Trained Puppy class."

Mrs Trigg opened the door and smiled at them. "Hello," she said, wiping her hands on her apron. "How did the training session go?"

"It was OK," said Max. He started to fidget,

looking very excited. Mandy wondered what was going on.

Max glanced from his gran to Mandy, and then down at Holly. "You know what, Gran? I've just had a brilliant idea!"

Everyone stared at him.

"What is it, Max?" asked Mrs Trigg.

"Why doesn't *Mandy* enter the Best Trained Puppy class with Holly?" Max burst out. "Then Holly could take part, even though you're going to be busy on the stall."

Mandy's heart leaped. She'd love to take part in the show with Holly! It would be just like having a dog of her own. But Holly was Mrs Trigg's dog, and it was up to her whether she wanted to enter Holly in the show or not. Mandy bent down to stroke Holly's smooth silky head, and looked up at Mrs Trigg.

Max's gran was smiling. "I think that's a splendid idea, Max," she beamed. "If Mandy would like to do it, that is."

"Oh, Mrs Trigg, I'd love to!" Mandy gasped.

5

Blackie in danger

"We've finished filling the gooseberry tarts, Gran," Mandy said, putting down her spoon. "What do you want us to do next?"

"Just give me a minute to pop this pie in the oven, and I'll tell you," said Grandma Hope. She opened the oven door and a blast of warm air filled the kitchen. "Is Blackie all right?"

James glanced under the kitchen table. "He's still chewing that bone you gave him, Mrs Hope," he said.

"As long as he's not chewing anything else!" Gran laughed. "Now, where are my oven gloves? I think this one's done now."

It was Thursday of the following week, and the dog show was only four days away. Mandy and James had come round to Lilac Cottage to give Gran a hand with the last batch of baking for the WI stall.

"I don't know where your grandad's got to," Gran went on. "I only sent him out for a bit of shopping, and he's been ages." She put the cooked pie on the worktop to cool. "How was your training session this morning, by the way?"

"Well, Holly was brilliant," said James. "Sandy was good, and Blackie was hopeless as usual."

"Oh, James, he wasn't!" Mandy said. "He did sit down when you told him to."

"Yes, for about a second!" James complained crossly. "And he still ignores me when I tell him to come to heel."

"Never mind," Mandy's gran said comfortingly. "There's still a few days before the show. Now, would you mind popping out into the lane and picking me some blackberries from the hedge?"

"Oh, Gran, are you going to make one of your yummy apple and blackberry pies?" Mandy asked.

Grandma Hope shook her head. "No, you'll have to wait and see," she said mysteriously, handing Mandy a plastic tub.

"What about Blackie?" asked James, bending down to check that the puppy was still under the table with his bone.

"Don't worry, I'll keep an eye on him," replied Gran.

Mandy and James went out through the back garden. There was a lane running behind the cottages where blackberries grew wild. The brambles were covered with juicy, dark purple berries. Mandy and James set to work.

"I don't think I'm ever going to get Blackie properly trained," grumbled James, dropping a handful of blackberries into the tub. "I wish he was as well-behaved as Holly."

"He'll get better," Mandy said. "I'm sure he will."

"Yes, but Holly *listens* to you," said James. "Half the time Blackie doesn't even seem to hear me! Then I get cross, and that doesn't help either."

"Perhaps you need to take Blackie to puppy training classes," Mandy suggested.

James sighed. "Maybe."

Mandy peered into the tub. "I wonder if we've picked enough yet," she said. "Let's go and ask Gran. And we can get a drink too. I'm really thirsty."

"Me too," James agreed. They went into the garden through the back gate, and into the kitchen. Grandma Hope wasn't there, but Mandy could hear her voice out in the hall.

"Gran must be on the phone," she said, putting the tub of blackberries on the table. "Do you want orange or lemon squash, James?"

James didn't reply. He was on his knees, staring under the table. "Where's Blackie?" he said, his voice sounding muffled.

"I don't know." Mandy glanced round the

kitchen. "Maybe he's in the hall with Gran."

James went to look, and came back shaking his head. "He's not in the garden, either," he said, "or we would have seen him. Where can he be?"

"Ssh!" Mandy clutched James's arm. "Can you hear that noise?"

James pointed at the larder in the corner of the kitchen. "It sounds like it's coming from over there."

Grandma Hope's larder was a big cupboard with lots of shelves and enough space to walk right in. Mandy and James hurried over and looked inside.

Blackie was crouched on the floor, surrounded by bits of paper and silver foil. He was panting and shaking, and his body was heaving as if he was trying to be sick.

"Blackie!" James cried anxiously. "What have you been eating?" He bent down and picked up a small block of dark chocolate. There were teethmarks all over it.

"No wonder you feel sick, you silly thing." James bent down and gently stroked Blackie's head. "You've eaten three huge bars of Mrs Hope's cooking chocolate, by the look of it!"

He glanced up at Mandy. "He must have managed to knock the bars off one of the shelves. I hope your gran isn't going to be cross, especially after what happened with the marrow."

Mandy was staring at Blackie. *Chocolate is poisonous to dogs*, she remembered her dad saying once. *It's dangerous because it can affect a dog's heart and nervous system . . .*

"James, stay with Blackie," she said urgently. Her heart lurched as she looked down at the puppy. He was shaking even more now. "I'm going to call Animal Ark."

"OK," said James, putting his arm round Blackie. "He does look ill, doesn't he? Still, he'll be all right soon, I suppose."

"James, chocolate is poisonous for dogs if they eat too much of it," Mandy burst out. "Blackie might be very ill!"

James's eyes widened as he stared at Mandy, trying to take in what she'd told him. "You mean – Blackie might *die*?" he whispered, his face turning white.

"We need to get him to Animal Ark as soon as we can," Mandy said, turning round and hurrying out of the kitchen. *Please let Blackie be OK*, she thought.

Grandma Hope had just finished her call and was hanging up the receiver. "What on earth is the matter, Mandy?" she exclaimed when she saw the look on Mandy's face.

"It's Blackie!" Mandy gasped. "He got into the larder and ate too much chocolate and now he's really ill. I have to phone Dad at Animal Ark."

Gran looked shocked. "Of course, love, call him right away. Oh, this is all my fault. I shouldn't have been so long on the phone." And she hurried down the hall towards the kitchen.

Mandy's fingers shook as she dialled the familiar number. She glanced at the clock. Her mum and dad would probably be at home, unless they'd been called out to an emergency . . .

Mandy gripped the receiver hard as the phone at Animal Ark began to ring.

"Hello?"

"Dad!" Mandy almost cried with relief. "Can you come to Lilac Cottage? Blackie's eaten three bars of cooking chocolate and he looks really ill."

Mandy heard her dad gasp at the other end of the line. "Has he been sick yet?" Mr Hope asked quickly.

"No, but he looks like he's going to be," Mandy replied.

"I'll be right there," said her dad, and hung up.

Mandy ran back into the kitchen. James was cradling Blackie in his arms, looking very scared. Blackie was panting heavily and trembling. Behind them, Gran was mopping the floor of the larder.

"Blackie was sick just now," James explained. He looked hopefully up at Mandy. "Maybe that will help."

"Yes, it should do," Mandy agreed. But Blackie had eaten such a lot of chocolate that she wasn't sure being sick once would make much difference.

It seemed to take ages for Mr Hope to arrive. Mandy kept dashing into the living-room to look for him, leaving James and Gran with Blackie. When she saw the Land-rover pull up outside, she immediately ran to open the front door.

"Where is he, love?" asked Adam Hope as he hurried inside, carrying his vet bag.

"In the larder with James and Gran." Mandy's voice wobbled. "Dad, he looks really ill."

"Well, let's see what we can do," her dad said comfortingly.

Blackie had been sick again, and now he lay with his head in James's lap, his eyes wide open and anxious.

"How long ago did Blackie eat the chocolate?" asked Mr Hope, kneeling down next to James.

Mandy thought hard. "James and I were picking blackberries," she said. "And then we had to wait for you to get here. It must have been about an hour ago."

"An hour," Mandy's dad repeated. "It's too late for me to give him salt water to make him sick, then. Let's just get this little fellow back to Animal Ark." He lifted Blackie very gently. "Mandy, will you carry my bag for me?"

"Mr Hope?" James scrambled to his feet. "Blackie *will* be all right, won't he?"

Adam Hope's face was very grave. "I'm afraid I don't know, James," he said.

"Call me as soon as there's any news," Grandma Hope said anxiously, following them down the hall.

"We will," Mandy promised.

She felt as if she was in the middle of a horrible nightmare as her dad drove them to Animal Ark. James didn't say a word. He just sat stroking Blackie, who lay next to him on the back seat.

When they arrived, Mr Hope rushed

Blackie straight into the surgery. "I'm going to give Blackie a sedative injection first, James," he explained as he put the trembling puppy on to the examining table. "That will help to slow his heart rate down."

James nodded, his face as white as a sheet. Mandy felt very sorry for him.

"Chocolate has two ingredients that are poisonous to dogs," Mr Hope went on, moving over to the cupboard in the corner. "They're called caffeine and theobromine. The sedative will help to fight them. And I'm going to put Blackie on a drip to replace the water he has lost being sick."

"Will he be all right after that?" asked James, biting his lip.

"I'm sorry, James," Mr Hope said gently, "but we won't know for sure until this time tomorrow."

James turned to Mandy. "I wish I hadn't got so cross with Blackie about the training," he said miserably. "That doesn't matter now. He might not even be able to take part in the show at all . . ." His voice shook.

"Oh, James!" Mandy said, swallowing a huge lump in her throat. She couldn't bear to see her friend looking so upset. Blackie *had* to get well again. He simply *had* to.

6

A hairy problem

"I can't stand all this waiting," James muttered as he stroked Blackie's head.

"Well, we'll soon know if Blackie's OK," Mandy said. "Won't we, Dad?"

It was the following morning. James had arrived at Animal Ark very early to check on Blackie, who had spent the night in the residential unit. The puppy was still asleep, curled up on a fleecy blanket.

Adam Hope nodded. "Yes, I just need to run a few tests," he replied. "Blackie's condition is stable, which means he isn't getting any worse. That's a good sign, but I have to make sure there's no lasting damage."

James looked very worried.

"I'll let you know as soon as I have any news," Mr Hope promised.

"Thanks, Dad," Mandy said. "We thought we'd walk over to Holly Cottage and see Max while you're doing Blackie's tests." She had rung Max yesterday to tell him about Blackie, and he'd been very shocked and upset.

James gave Blackie one last pat. Then he and Mandy left Animal Ark and set off through Welford.

"I don't care *how* naughty Blackie is, as long as he gets well again," James sighed as they headed towards Holly Cottage.

"He'll be fine," Mandy said confidently, hoping she was right.

Max was looking out for them. He flung open the front door as they walked up the path. "How's Blackie?" he demanded.

"He's still asleep," replied James. "He looks

a bit better, but Mr Hope's got to do some tests."

"Where's Sandy?" Mandy asked.

Max's face turned pink. "In the living-room," he mumbled, sounding a bit embarrassed. "You'd better come in."

Mandy wondered what was wrong. As they went into the living-room, Sandy looked up from where he was sitting on the rug. Mandy hardly recognised him. "Max!" she cried, her eyes widening as she stared at the Cairn terrier. "What's happened to Sandy's coat?"

The puppy looked like a little ball of pale gold fluff. His fur was completely frizzy and stuck out all over.

"I just wanted him to look good for the show," Max explained sheepishly. "So I gave him a bath and dried him with Gran's hairdryer."

Mandy couldn't help laughing, and even James smiled.

"Didn't he mind the noise of the hairdryer?" Mandy asked, bending down to pat the fluffy little puppy. "Oh!" She gasped as her hand touched Sandy's coat. Instead of being soft, it felt hard and crunchy. And Sandy smelled rather strange, too!

Max looked even more embarrassed. "I used some of Gran's hairspray after I'd dried him," he admitted. "But I don't think Sandy likes it very much."

Sandy gave a high-pitched bark, as if he agreed with Max. Then he began to scratch his ears vigorously with one of his paws.

"He's been doing that all morning," said Max. "I don't know what's wrong with him."

Mandy looked at the frizzy little dog, who was still scratching madly. "I wonder if it's the hairspray," she said. "It might be making his skin itchy."

Max looked horrified. "Really? I hadn't thought of that."

"Maybe you'd better give him another bath," Mandy suggested.

Max sighed. "I don't think Gran will be very pleased," he said. "We made a bit of a mess this morning!"

Mandy thought for a moment. "Why don't you bring Sandy to Animal Ark, and we can wash him there?" she said. "Mum and Dad have got some proper pet shampoo in the surgery. I'm sure they'll let us use some."

"And I can check on Blackie," added James.

"OK, I'll just go and ask Gran," said Max, and he dashed off into the garden.

Sandy scratched his ear again and sniffed at his coat suspiciously. Then he stared glumly up at Mandy and James, as if to say *I don't recognise this smell at all!*

"Gran said that's fine," Max said breathlessly, arriving back in the living-room with Sandy's lead. "I hope the hairspray hasn't hurt Sandy," he added anxiously.

"He'll probably be fine when you've

washed it off," Mandy said. "But if you're worried, we can ask Mum and Dad about it."

They set off for Animal Ark, although it took them a bit longer than usual because Sandy kept stopping to have a good scratch. James was very quiet, and Mandy knew he was thinking about Blackie. She felt nervous, too. Would her dad have good news for them?

Morning surgery had just finished when they arrived at Animal Ark. Mandy's mum was standing in the surgery waiting room, chatting to Jean Knox, the receptionist.

"Mrs Hope, is there any news?" James asked quickly.

Emily Hope patted his shoulder. "Mandy's dad is doing those tests right now. He'll come and tell you the minute he's got anything to report."

"James, I'm so sorry about Blackie," Jean said sympathetically. Then she noticed Sandy standing next to Max. "Goodness me! Whatever's happened to Sandy?"

Mrs Hope bent down to look closely at the Cairn terrier. "That's funny," she said, sounding puzzled. "He smells of hairspray."

Max blushed as he explained what had happened.

"Well, you do need to wash the hairspray off," Mandy's mum said with a smile. "You can use our bathroom. And remember, it's never a good idea to use products meant for humans on dogs – or any animal!"

"I haven't hurt Sandy, have I?" Max asked anxiously.

Mrs Hope shook her head. "No, but use a dog shampoo this time." She took a bottle off the shelves beside the reception desk and handed it to Max.

"Thanks, Mum," Mandy said gratefully. "I promise we won't make too much mess!"

Max carried Sandy upstairs while James filled the bath and Mandy went to get an old towel to dry Sandy off afterwards. Sandy didn't look at all pleased to be having two baths in one day and he tried to wriggle out of Max's arms, but Max held on to him tightly.

"You're going to look great for the show, Sandy," Max told his puppy as he turned on the shower hose and began to wet Sandy's frizzy coat all over. "You'll have to stay nice and clean, though."

Mandy unscrewed the top of the shampoo bottle. "At least the weather's OK," she said. "We haven't had any rain for ages, so there aren't any puddles for Sandy to roll around in."

"Don't speak too soon," said James, pointing at the window. "I think it's raining right now!"

They all looked outside. James was right. The rain was very light, so they hadn't heard it at first. But it was getting heavier.

Max groaned. "Sandy's coat is difficult enough to keep clean already," he grumbled. "And it's even worse when the weather's bad. I'm going to have to carry him everywhere!"

"Or buy him some little wellies," joked James.

"Mm, this smells nice," Mandy said, tipping some of the green shampoo into her hands. "I don't think Sandy likes it though!"

Sandy stretched his head round to sniff at the shampoo as Mandy began to rub it into his coat, and wrinkled his lip in disgust.

"It's much better for you than the hairspray, Sandy," Max promised.

James turned on the taps again, and they rinsed Sandy with the shower hose until every speck of shampoo was washed away. The strong-smelling foam ran off his coat in steady streams, leaving Sandy's fur damp and slick against his body. Max lifted the puppy out of the bath, but before Mandy had a chance to wrap the towel round him, Sandy decided to give himself a good shake.

"Sandy!" yelled Max as drops of water flew everywhere.

"I'm soaked," Mandy laughed.

"We're almost as wet as Sandy is!" added James.

Suddenly Mandy heard footsteps coming up the stairs. She turned to James, feeling anxious. "I think that's Dad."

James jumped to his feet, looking pale.

The bathroom door opened and Mr Hope came in. To Mandy's utter relief, he was smiling. "Blackie's going to be fine, James," he said. "His heart rate's down and he's looking much brighter."

"Really?" gasped James, his eyes shining.

Mandy and Max beamed at each other in delight.

Mr Hope nodded. "He'll need to stick to very simple food for a while. Boiled chicken and rice, that sort of thing. But he'll be back to normal in a day or so. He'll even be able to take part in the dog show if you want."

"Can I see him?" asked James.

"Of course," smiled Mandy's dad. "And remember, it's special doggy chocs only for Blackie from now on! Doggy chocolate doesn't have the dangerous ingredients that human chocolate has."

"You go with James, Mandy," Max offered. "I'll come down when I've dried Sandy."

Mandy flew down the stairs after James and her dad, a broad grin on her face. She felt like singing at the top of her voice. Blackie was going to be OK!

Blackie was lying on his blanket in the residential unit. James crouched down and stroked his soft black head, and Blackie licked his owner's hand in response. His tail thumped softly against the floor of the cage.

"Isn't it *great*, Mandy?" James said happily.

Mandy nodded.

"And I don't care how naughty he is now," James added, tickling his puppy gently under the chin. "Blackie's all right, and that's all that matters."

7

Dogs galore!

"Look, Mum! The sun's coming out," Mandy announced as she went into the kitchen. It was the day of the dog show, and since Blackie's recovery it had rained heavily every single day. It had rained earlier that morning too, but now Mandy had spotted a patch of clear blue sky.

"We'll still have to wear our wellies,"

warned Mrs Hope. "The grass is going to be very wet."

Mandy nodded. The dog show was taking place in a large field just outside Welford, and lots of visitors were expected. The ground would be very muddy. Mandy just hoped that they would be able to keep the three dogs clean until their classes took place. "Is it time to go now, Mum?" she asked eagerly.

Mrs Hope had already dropped Mandy's dad off at the field so that he had time to prepare the vet's tent before the show started.

Mandy's mum laughed and looked at the clock. "Yes, all right," she agreed. "But put your wellies on first!"

Mandy quickly got ready and followed her mum out to the Land-rover. They were stopping off to collect James, Max and the three dogs on their way to the show. Mrs Trigg had left earlier to help with the WI stall, so Max, Sandy and Holly had gone round to the Hunters' house.

"I wonder how Blackie will get on this afternoon," said Mrs Hope as she started up the engine.

"I don't think James minds," Mandy

replied. "He's just so glad that Blackie's OK."

"Yes, it was a nasty scare," said her mum. "And Blackie didn't help himself by being so greedy!"

They pulled up outside the Hunters' house. Straight away the door opened and Blackie shot out at top speed.

"Blackie!" yelled James, appearing in the doorway. "Come back!"

"Oh yes, I can see that Blackie is *definitely* back to normal!" laughed Mrs Hope.

Grinning, Mandy slipped out of her seat and bent down to make a fuss of Blackie. "I've got him, James," she called, as Blackie licked her nose lovingly.

James and Max came out of the house and hurried towards the Land-rover. James had Holly on her lead, and Max was carrying Sandy, stepping carefully over the puddles on the path.

"Hi, Mrs Hope," said James as he climbed into the Land-rover. "Thanks for giving us a lift."

"Do you think it's going to rain again?" asked Max, peering out of the car window.

"Well, there's more blue sky every

minute," Mrs Hope pointed out. "I think it will stay fine."

"How's Blackie been?" Mandy asked, hugging Holly who was sitting quietly on her lap. Blackie had been allowed home on Saturday afternoon after Mr Hope had given him a final check-up.

"Oh, he's fine," said James. "Back to his naughty old self!"

"I didn't know chocolate was so bad for dogs," Max said solemnly. "I'm going to be really careful what I give Sandy from now on."

"That's a very sensible idea," Mrs Hope agreed.

A few minutes later they arrived at the dog show. Mandy leaned out of the window, looking around eagerly. The field was full of tents and stalls, and there were already lots of people around – and dogs!

Mandy had never *seen* so many dogs in one place before. "Oh, look at that St Bernard!" she exclaimed, as a massive brown and white dog ambled past with his owner. "Isn't he gorgeous?"

"And look at those three Westies," Max

added. "They're really white. I wonder how their owner manages to keep *them* clean."

Mrs Hope parked the Land-rover in the car park and they all climbed out. Mandy was glad that the organisers of the show had put down wooden boards for people to walk on where the grass was really muddy.

Max was pleased too. "Now I won't have to carry Sandy all the time," he said thankfully.

"What shall we do first, Mum?" asked Mandy. "Shall we go and see Dad or Gran?"

"The vet's tent is over there," said James, who had spotted the sign.

"Let's pop in and see your dad," suggested Mrs Hope. "We don't have a lot of time, because the Best Trained Puppy class is first on the schedule. We'll go and see your gran in the WI tent when the class is over."

They walked over to the vet's tent. Mandy went in first, with Holly trotting next to her. She was amazed to see two huge black dogs with thick, shaggy coats standing in the middle of the tent, all on their own. "Oh!" Mandy clapped her hand to her mouth.

Behind her, Blackie and Sandy began

growling. Holly looked a bit nervous too.

To Mandy's surprise, her dad suddenly popped up on the other side of the shaggy black dogs. So did another man, whom Mandy didn't recognise.

"Hello, did we startle you?" said Mr Hope with a grin. "These lovely fellows belong to Mr Hawkins here. Come and say hello."

"Oh, they're gorgeous," Mandy said admiringly. The dogs were standing very patiently, even though Blackie and Sandy were still growling at them.

"Be quiet, Blackie," James scolded. "Those dogs could gobble you up for breakfast!"

Mr Hawkins laughed. He was a short, plump man wearing gold-rimmed glasses and a smart navy-blue suit. "Julius and Cleopatra wouldn't hurt a fly," he said, smoothing the dogs' backs. "They're gentle giants, really, like all Newfoundlands."

"Can we stroke them?" Mandy asked.

Mr Hawkins nodded, so Mandy, James and Max went over to pat the dogs. They were broad and muscular, and their coats were thick and very soft. Mandy thought it felt like burying her fingers in a warm, cosy rug.

"You must have to groom them all the time," remarked James, running his hands over Cleopatra's back.

"Well, it is quite hard work, especially during the show season!" Mr Hawkins agreed with a laugh. Then he glanced at his watch. "Goodness me, is that the time? I must go and open the show. Everybody will be waiting!" And he hurried out of the tent, with Julius and Cleopatra padding calmly alongside him.

"Mr Hawkins is the president of the show," Adam Hope told them, his eyes twinkling. "So he's a very busy person!"

"We'd better get a move on too," said Mrs Hope. "The classes start in ten minutes."

"Dad, will you be able to come and watch?" Mandy asked.

"I'm not sure, love, but I'll try," replied her dad. "Good luck, anyway."

They left the tent just in time to catch the end of Mr Hawkins' opening speech. He was standing on a small platform in the middle of Ring One, with Julius and Cleopatra sitting on either side of him.

"And do remember that all the profits we

make today are going to local dog charities," he was saying. "So spend as much money as you like!" Everyone laughed. "I now declare the Seven Dales Dog Show open," Mr Hawkins went on. "And those of you who are taking part in the Best Trained Puppy class, please make your way to Ring Four immediately. This class is about to start. Thank you."

Mandy felt a ripple of excitement run through her. But she was nervous too, because she wanted to do well for Mrs Trigg. "We'd better go over to the ring," Mandy said, glancing down at Holly. At least she didn't look nervous! Holly didn't even seem to mind all the people milling around them.

"This way, then," said Mrs Hope.

Mandy glanced at James and Max as they followed her mum. Max looked a bit pale, but James didn't seem worried at all. He was too busy ruffling Blackie's ears and smiling down at his puppy.

There were a lot of people making their way over to the ring. Some of them were going to watch, while others were competing with their dogs. Mandy spotted Mrs

Ponsonby, who lived at Bleakfell Hall just outside Welford, with her pampered Pekinese, Pandora. Mandy grinned to herself. Maybe there should be a class for Best Trained Owners! Pandora certainly had the knack of making Mrs Ponsonby do whatever she wanted – feed her tasty snacks, carry her if her legs got tired, dress her in little jackets when it was cold!

"Ah, there you are!" said a familiar voice. Mandy looked round and saw Grandad Hope walking towards them. He had a paper bag in his hand.

"Your gran's stall is doing a roaring trade," he said. "You'll have to go and see her when your class is over." He grinned at Mandy, James and Max. "She's got a surprise for you!"

"Oh, what is it, Grandad?" Mandy asked.

"You'll have to wait and see," replied Grandad, his eyes twinkling. "Do you want an oatmeal biscuit?" he went on, holding out the paper bag. "They're from the WI stall."

Blackie lifted his head to sniff the air, looking very interested. He launched himself at Grandad's legs with a loud bark, tail wagging.

"Blackie, you can't have any!" James scolded him. "You're only supposed to have rice and chicken at the moment."

"Actually, a little bit of oatmeal biscuit wouldn't hurt him," said Mandy's mum.

Grandad gave Blackie a small piece of biscuit, which he gulped down as if he hadn't been fed for a week. Holly and Sandy nudged Grandad's legs, looking hopeful, so they got a piece too.

"There's a lot of people here," said Emily Hope, glancing round the ring. "I think we'd

better go and find some seats. Good luck, all of you." And she and Grandad went off.

As they waited outside the ring, Mandy noticed a tall, thin woman wearing a floaty white dress and a big white hat with a pink ribbon round the crown. She was holding a spotless white poodle on a sparkly pink lead, with a pink ribbon around his neck that was exactly the same colour as the one on his owner's hat. The poodle's coat had been trimmed so that all he had left were ruffs of fur around his legs, neck and tummy. Mandy couldn't help staring.

James nudged Mandy. "I don't like it when people do that to poodles, do you?" he whispered in her ear.

Mandy didn't like it much either. She always thought the dogs looked a bit cold. The poodle seemed quite nervous. He was jumping skittishly about, pulling on his lead and yapping at the other dogs.

"Rupert, will you behave yourself!" his owner said fussily.

Suddenly Rupert fixed his eyes on Sandy and began to growl. Mandy felt alarmed. She glanced over at Max. He'd spotted the poodle as well, and was trying to pull Sandy away from him. But there were too many people standing around for him to get away easily.

"Max, look out!" Mandy gasped as the poodle suddenly lunged towards Sandy.

Poor Sandy wasn't quite sure what was happening. He backed hastily away from the angry poodle, ears flat against his head, and splashed right into a large, muddy puddle. Rupert flew after him, yapping and growling, and dragging his owner with him.

"Sandy!" Max yelled frantically, trying to pull his puppy out of the puddle, and out of reach of Rupert, too.

Mandy watched in horror as the poodle launched itself at Sandy, his teeth bared. Was Sandy going to get hurt?

8

Best Trained Puppies

For a few seconds, there was mayhem. Mandy wanted to go and help Max and Sandy, but she had to hang on to Holly, who was barking furiously. James was having the same problem with Blackie. Dogs were barking and growling all around them.

"Somebody do something!" shrieked Mrs Ponsonby, clutching her precious Pandora in her arms. Mandy wished Mrs Ponsonby would stop screaming. She was just making things worse.

"Leave my Rupert alone!" shouted the furious poodle owner, jabbing her umbrella at Sandy. She was red in the face and her hat had slipped over one eye.

"But it wasn't Sandy's fault," Max protested.

With one big tug on the lead, the woman managed to drag Rupert away from Sandy. Other people began to move off, trying to calm their dogs. Mandy let out a shaky sigh of relief. Everything seemed to have stopped as quickly as it had started, although Sandy was still cowering, wet and dirty, behind Max's legs.

"Sandy, are you OK?" Max asked anxiously. He picked the puppy up and cuddled him, not bothering about the muddy water that dripped all over his clean sweatshirt.

"That dog's a menace!" Rupert's owner announced crossly, pointing at Sandy with her umbrella. "A dangerous animal like that shouldn't be allowed at the show."

Mandy couldn't bear to hear Sandy accused

of being dangerous. "That's not fair," she burst out. "Sandy didn't do anything."

Rupert's owner ignored her. "I'm going to make sure you're disqualified!" she snapped.

"Excuse me," said a deep voice. Mandy, James and Max turned round to see Mr Hawkins standing behind them, looking stern. Mandy's heart sank. Surely Mr Hawkins wasn't going to tell Sandy and Max to leave the show?

"I saw exactly what happened," Mr Hawkins went on, staring hard at Rupert's owner. "It wasn't Sandy's fault at all."

"That's very true," Mrs Ponsonby agreed loudly over Mandy's shoulder. "That poodle attacked Max Trigg's dog first."

Mandy felt very relieved. It looked as though Sandy wasn't going to be blamed after all!

"I think you'd better take Rupert home," added Mr Hawkins. "I don't think we can allow him to compete today, after what's happened."

Rupert's owner hurried away, very shamefaced, with Rupert trotting meekly beside her.

Max gave a sigh of relief. "Thanks, Mr Hawkins," he said. Then he looked at his bedraggled puppy and his face fell. "But I don't think Sandy and I will be taking part in the show either," he sighed. "Look at him!"

"We can clean him up," Mandy said.

Mr Hawkins nodded. "Of course you can. I've brought my dogs' grooming equipment with me," he told Max. "You can use my brushes. And I'm sure I can get you some hot water from the refreshments tent."

Max brightened up. "Really?"

"Will all competitors in the Best Trained Puppy class please make their way into the ring immediately?" said a voice over the tannoy.

"You two go ahead," Max told Mandy and James. "Sandy and I won't make it in time for this class."

"Never mind, you've still got the Best Terrier class later," Mandy reminded him.

Mr Hawkins took Max off to the vet's tent to get Sandy cleaned up, while Mandy and James hurried over to the ring to join the other competitors. Mandy was pleased to see Joey Appleyard and his dog Scruff among them. Joey, who was in Mandy's class at school, was deaf, and Mandy and James had helped him train Scruff to be his hearing dog. As the names of the competitors and their dogs were read out, Mandy waved at Joey, and he grinned back at her.

"This is it, Holly," Mandy murmured nervously. She bent down to stroke the little dog's velvety ears. Holly licked her fingers. She looked very solemn, almost as if she understood that she had to be on her best behaviour.

"Right, we would like you to walk round the ring, please," said one of the judges, a short, dark-haired man with a beard. Mandy saw that Joey was watching the judge very closely so that he could lip-read the instructions.

The puppies set off, led by Mandy and Holly. Holly was behaving beautifully, Mandy thought proudly. The little dog trotted quietly along, matching her pace to Mandy's and not pulling on her lead at all. Behind her, though, Mandy could hear James whispering to Blackie.

"Blackie, stop it! *Blackie!*"

Mandy didn't dare look round because the judges were watching them. She just hoped Blackie wasn't being *too* naughty.

When all the competitors had paraded round the ring, the judges asked them to stand in line. It was time for each of them to do an individual show. Mandy and Holly were first. Her heart beating hard, Mandy waited for the signal from the judges to begin. She knew that they would be watching carefully, and giving points not just for Holly's obedience, but for her own skill at handling the puppy.

Holly stood patiently beside her, her warm body pressed comfortingly against Mandy's legs.

Mandy glanced round the audience. There were her mum and Grandad. Mandy beamed at them. Her dad was watching too, standing next to the ring entrance. He must have popped out of the vet's tent to see the class. It was a shame Mrs Trigg couldn't be there to see Holly perform, though.

First, Mandy showed the judges how Holly could walk to heel, both on and off her lead. Holly stuck to Mandy's heels like glue, following her round the ring. When they stopped, Mandy suddenly noticed Mrs Trigg sitting next to Grandad. Mandy felt very pleased. Max's gran had managed to get away to watch Holly after all!

Mandy soon forgot there were lots of people watching. She was concentrating so hard, it felt like she and Holly were the only ones there. Holly kept glancing up at Mandy, her big dark eyes fixed on Mandy's face, as if she was saying *You just tell me what to do, and I'll do it!*

"Sit, Holly," Mandy said.

Holly sat immediately.

"Stay," Mandy told her. She walked across to the other side of the ring. When she turned round, Holly was still sitting in the same place, watching her with her head on one side.

"Come, Holly!" Mandy called, patting her knees. Holly bounded across the ring, her feathery tail wagging joyously. As Mandy bent down and hugged her, the audience clapped loudly.

Mandy's heart was still thumping hard as she clipped Holly's lead to her collar, but she felt very pleased. She knew that Holly had done really well! And she could see Mrs Trigg smiling proudly as she led Holly back to join the line of competitors.

"You were brilliant," whispered James.

"You mean *Holly* was brilliant!" Mandy replied, stroking the little dog.

Joey Appleyard and Scruff were next, and Mandy watched intently as the two of them performed. There really was an incredible bond between Joey and his dog. Scruff never took his eyes off Joey for a moment and seemed to be able to tell exactly what his owner was thinking. The puppy was so quick at responding to Joey's commands, it was almost like magic.

Mandy smiled when she spotted Mrs Appleyard, Joey's mum, sitting in the audience looking very proud. At first Mrs Appleyard hadn't wanted Joey to adopt Scruff, because she was scared of dogs. Now she loved Scruff almost as much as Joey did.

There were several other entrants after Joey and Scruff, then it was James and Blackie's turn.

"I'm a bit nervous," James confessed as he walked forwards with Blackie.

"You'll be fine!" Mandy whispered.

Blackie bounced along beside James, looking very pleased with himself. It wasn't a bad start, Mandy thought hopefully.

Suddenly Blackie's ears pricked up and his tail began to wag furiously. He'd spotted Grandad Hope in the front row. Mandy groaned as Blackie lunged towards Grandad, dragging James with him. Blackie must have thought he was going to get another delicious biscuit!

"Blackie, no!" hissed James, his face going a bright shade of scarlet.

The audience thought this was very funny and roared with laughter. But that just seemed to encourage Blackie. The puppy yanked the lead right out of James's hand, raced towards Grandad and Mrs Hope, and tried to scramble under the ropes to get to them. James had to kneel down and grab hold of Blackie's collar to haul him back into the ring.

Then, when James tried to make Blackie sit and stay, the puppy leaped up and dashed after James as soon as he walked away. James tried to tell him off, but Blackie melted everyone's heart by looking very sheepish and sitting up and begging. Mandy felt a bit sorry for James, who was looking really embarrassed by now, but Blackie was the star of the show!

"That was awful!" James puffed, as he rejoined the line with Blackie jumping around happily beside him. The judges were deep in discussion, looking at their clipboards and comparing their notes on each competitor.

Mandy laughed. "It doesn't matter," she said. "Everyone loved you."

"Blackie, you're a bad boy!" said James, but he was smiling as he bent down to hug his puppy. "I shouldn't think we've won, though. Not unless there's a prize for the naughtiest puppy!"

The judge with the beard was ready to announce the winners. "First of all, we want to say how well trained all of the puppies were," he said. He glanced at Blackie and James, and raised his eyebrows. "Well, *most* of them!" he added, and the audience laughed. "But we do have a winner. First prize goes to Joey Appleyard and Scruff."

Mandy clapped loudly as Joey stepped forward, his eyes shining, to receive his rosette. She thought they really deserved it.

"And now for our second prize," the judge went on. "This goes to Mandy Hope and Holly!"

9
Gran's mystery jam

"Second prize!" Mandy gasped in delight. She shook hands with the judge, who fixed the big blue rosette to Holly's collar.

"You've obviously got a real bond with Holly," he said, patting the puppy on her head. "How long have you owned her?"

"Oh, Holly's not my dog," Mandy explained. "She belongs to my friend's gran."

"Really?" The judge looked surprised. "That's even more impressive, then. You did very well."

The third prize was presented to a boy with a handsome brown and white spaniel pup, and then the class was over. Mandy immediately led Holly over to her mum and Grandad. Max was standing next to them with Sandy, who was clean again.

"I knew you and Holly would do well!" cried Max, beaming at Mandy.

"Yes, you were marvellous," agreed Mrs Trigg, patting her prize-winning pup. Holly wagged her tail proudly. "I didn't get a chance to see the other dogs because I had to pop back to the stall." Mrs Trigg glanced at James, her eyes twinkling. "But I hear that Blackie caused quite a stir!"

James laughed. "I think we'll have to try again next year," he said.

Mandy's dad gave her a quick hug. "I'd better get back to the vet's tent," he said. "You were great, love."

"Let's go over and tell your gran," suggested Grandad Hope. "She was really disappointed that she couldn't get away to watch you and James."

"Yes, I'd better get back too," said Mrs Trigg.

"Will you come and watch me and Sandy later on, Gran?" asked Max, and Mrs Trigg nodded.

"Sandy looks much better now," Mandy told Max, patting the little dog.

"Yes, Mr Hawkins helped me groom him." Max sighed. "But his coat's still sticking up. I just hope the judges don't mind."

Grandad Hope led Mandy, James, Max and the three dogs over to the big tent where the WI stall was. Mandy's mum and Mrs Trigg followed them. Mandy could still hardly believe that she and Holly had come second. She couldn't wait to tell Gran!

The WI tent was packed with people. They were all crowded round Grandma Hope's stall, making it difficult for Mandy and the others to get close.

"What are all these people buying?" Max asked curiously, as a man in a tweed suit went past with his arms full of jars. Lots of other people seemed to be buying the same thing.

"It looks like some sort of jam," Mandy

replied, peering round to see. "Blackberry, maybe?"

"Mm, I can see some ginger snaps on that table over there," said Max. "Gran, can I buy some of those for my mum and dad?"

Mrs Trigg nodded. "I'll save you some," she said, and she squeezed past a tall lady in front of them to get back to her stall.

"Mandy!" Gran had spotted them over the heads of the customers, and was waving. "How did you get on?"

Mandy wriggled through the people and

found a space to stand in beside Gran's stall. "Holly and I came second," she announced proudly, bending down to smooth Holly's silky fur. The little dog twisted her head round and gave Mandy's hand a friendly lick.

"That's wonderful, love." Gran looked thrilled. "How about you, James?" she asked as James, Max and Grandad Hope appeared behind Mandy.

"It's probably better not to ask, Mrs Hope!" James joked, patting Blackie.

"Gran, what's that jam everyone's buying?" Mandy asked, as yet another customer went past, carrying two of the jars. They had handwritten labels on, but Mandy couldn't quite see what the labels said.

Gran glanced at Grandad and laughed. "Wait there," she said.

James grinned at Mandy. "Maybe it *is* blackberry jam," he said. "After all, we did pick all those blackberries!"

Gran slipped out from behind the table and came round to join them. She was carrying a plate of small pieces of bread spread with purple jam. "Because some of the things we've got for sale are quite unusual, we're giving people a taste before they buy," she explained. "This is the jam that everyone's going mad for!"

Mandy, James and Max each took a bit of bread.

"What's it like?" asked Emily Hope, taking a piece too.

"It's yummy!" Mandy announced. "It *is* blackberry jam, isn't it, Gran?"

Gran's eyes twinkled. "Not quite," she replied.

"Blackcurrant?" James guessed.

"Plum?" suggested Max.

Gran and Grandad smiled. "It's marrow and blackberry jam," Gran announced.

"*Marrow?*" Mandy repeated, amazed. "Gran! You used Grandad's marrow to make jam!"

Grandma Hope nodded. "And everyone seems to love it," she smiled. "I've sold so many jars, I'll be able to buy Grandad some more marrow seeds to plant *next* year."

"I told you it was a wonderful marrow," Grandad added proudly.

"James, it's almost time for the Handsomest Pup class to start," Emily Hope reminded him, as they all helped themselves to another sample of the blackberry and marrow jam.

"Oh, I almost forgot!" James exclaimed. "At least Blackie won't have to do too much this time."

"Except look handsome," Mandy laughed.

"I'd better not give him any titbits before *this* class!" Grandad Hope said with a smile.

They said goodbye to Grandma Hope and Mrs Trigg, and squeezed their way through the crowd and back to the ring. James and Blackie dashed off to join the other entrants, while Mandy sat down in the front row with her mum, Grandad Hope and Max. Holly and Sandy settled down comfortably at their feet.

"I hope Blackie behaves himself this time," Mandy whispered to Max as the owners and their dogs filed into the ring.

The names of the competitors were read out, and James and Blackie got an extra-loud round of applause. Mandy guessed that some of the audience had seen Blackie's performance earlier! Then the dogs began to walk round the ring with their owners. Blackie looked very handsome and healthy.

His coat was glossy and thick, and his eyes were bright. It was hard to believe he was the same puppy who'd been so ill just a few days ago. Mandy was relieved to see that Blackie seemed to have calmed down a bit too, and was walking round quite quietly. Once he tried to nip the tail of the German Shepherd puppy in front of him, but Mandy hoped that neither of the judges had noticed that.

Then it was time for the dogs to be checked over by the judges. Mandy watched, her heart

in her mouth, when it was Blackie's turn. He was very friendly, wagging his tail and wriggling, but at least he kept still long enough for the judges to look at his eyes and in his mouth.

As the judge stepped forward to announce the results, Mandy sat on the edge of her seat.

"And our winner is . . ." The judge paused and glanced round the audience. "Rocky, the German Shepherd, owned by Michael Green."

Everyone clapped as Rocky's owner stepped forward to receive a rosette and a large bag of dog biscuits. Second place went to a beautiful snow-white Westie. Mandy couldn't help feeling a bit disappointed that Blackie hadn't been mentioned so far.

The judge waited until the audience had stopped clapping. "And our third Handsomest Pup today is Blackie, owned by James Hunter."

"Oh!" Mandy gasped. "Well done, Blackie!" She clapped as hard as she could as James, pink with delight, stepped forward to collect Blackie's prize.

Mandy couldn't help laughing when she

saw what it was. "Look, Max," she said. "Blackie's won a box of *doggy chocolates!*"

10

Showtime for Sandy

"Good luck, Max," said Mandy. "We'll cheer really loudly for you and Sandy."

"Thanks," Max replied. He bent down and ran his hands over Sandy's coat again, trying to smooth it down. It was no use – it still stuck out all over the place. Max shrugged and pulled a face. Then he led Sandy off to join the other entrants in the Best Terrier class. Mandy settled back in her seat next to James.

"No, Blackie," James scolded as the puppy sniffed hungrily at the box of doggy chocolates for the hundredth time. "You'll have to wait until your tummy's better."

"But special doggy chocolate will be fine for Blackie in a day or two," Mrs Hope added with a smile.

Just then Mrs Trigg arrived. "I haven't missed Max and Sandy, have I?" she puffed. "I ran all the way from the WI tent."

"It's OK, the class is just starting now," replied Grandad Hope.

Mandy watched as the dogs walked round the ring. Because it was a class for best terrier, there were several different breeds, including a tiny black and tan Yorkshire terrier and two lively Jack Russells. But Sandy was the only Cairn terrier.

Sandy behaved very well. He trotted obediently round the ring next to Max, and stood quietly when he was examined by the judges. Mandy could see that Max was still trying to flatten the puppy's fur with his hand.

She hoped that Sandy's sticking-up coat wouldn't count against him.

One of the judges was the man with a beard who had presented Mandy and Holly with their Best Trained Puppy rosette. When all the terriers had been examined, he stepped into the middle of the ring, holding his clipboard against his chest. "We had a very difficult decision to make in this class," he announced, clearing his throat, "but at last we have a winner. It's Sandy, owned by Max Trigg."

Mandy and James leaped to their feet, cheering at the top of their voices. Holly and Blackie joined in too, barking loudly, as Max accepted his rosette with a huge grin.

As soon as the other rosettes had been handed out and all the competitors filed out of the ring, Max rushed over to them, Sandy in his arms.

His gran gave him a hug. "Well done, love," she said.

"Hey! We've *all* won a prize!" Mandy suddenly realised. She looked at the three puppies, each proudly wearing their rosette – blue for Holly, yellow for Blackie, and red for Sandy. "Isn't that brilliant?"

"I can't believe it!" Max exclaimed, his eyes shining. "I really didn't think I would win, not after I had to wash Sandy again, and his coat was sticking up so much."

Someone laughed behind them, and Mandy looked round to see Mr Hawkins, the president of the dog show committee. "Well done, Max," he smiled. "Didn't you know that Cairn terriers are *supposed* to have coarse, sticking-up coats? And Sandy's is a very fine example!"

"No, I didn't," Max admitted. He rubbed his cheek against Sandy's soft fur. "But I should have known. After all, Sandy is the *Best* Terrier! Oh, and thank you for helping me to get Sandy cleaned up."

"Don't mention it," replied Mr Hawkins. "There's a reporter here from the *Walton Gazette*. She wants to take a picture of all the prize-winners, so you'd better go back into the ring."

"Come on," Max said to Mandy and James. Proudly, they led their dogs into the ring, where the reporter was trying to round up everyone who had won prizes. Mandy

recognised her. It was Alison West, who'd been at the County Show when Jenny and Tilly won the Dexter cow and calf class.

"Hello, Mandy," said Alison. "Did you win a prize today?"

"Yes, and so did my friends, Max and James," Mandy explained.

Alison smiled at the three dogs. "What lovely puppies!" she said. "I think you should all be at the front of the photo. Come and stand over here."

It took a while to get the other prize-

winners lined up behind Mandy, James and Max, but at last everyone was in place.

"Smile!" called Alison, lifting her camera.

Mandy beamed. It wasn't hard to smile after such a brilliant day. Three gorgeous puppies and three prizes! Mandy rested her hand on Holly's silky head, and the pup licked her fingers lovingly. In a few more days Mandy would be back at school, but she'd *never* forget these summer holidays – the best she'd ever had!

RAT RIDDLE
Animal Ark Pets 18

Lucy Daniels

Mandy and James's school-friend Martin has been given a pair of fancy rats for his birthday. Cheddar and Pickle love to race around their 'Incredible Rat Run'. At first, Mandy finds that Pickle is the fastest. But then Pickle's times begin to slow down. Could something be wrong?

FOAL FROLICS
Animal Ark Pets Summer Special

Lucy Daniels

Mandy and James are on holiday with Mandy's family. All sorts of things are disappearing from the campsite, and now golf balls from the nearby golf course are going missing too. It's a mystery until Mandy and James catch the thief red-handed: a cheeky foal called Mischief! The bad-tempered groundsman at the golf course wants Mischief removed. Can Mandy and James find a way for the foal to stay?

LUCY DANIELS
Animal Ark Pets

0 340 67283 8	Puppy Puzzle	£3.99	❏
0 340 67284 6	Kitten Crowd	£3.99	❏
0 340 67285 4	Rabbit Race	£3.99	❏
0 340 67286 2	Hamster Hotel	£3.99	❏
0 340 68729 0	Mouse Magic	£3.99	❏
0 340 68730 4	Chick Challenge	£3.99	❏
0 340 68731 2	Pony Parade	£3.99	❏
0 340 68732 0	Guinea-pig Gang	£3.99	❏
0 340 71371 2	Gerbil Genius	£3.99	❏
0 340 71372 0	Duckling Diary	£3.99	❏
0 340 71373 9	Lamb Lessons	£3.99	❏
0 340 71374 7	Doggy Dare	£3.99	❏
0 340 73585 6	Donkey Derby	£3.99	❏
0 340 73586 4	Hedgehog Home	£3.99	❏
0 340 73587 2	Frog Friends	£3.99	❏
0 340 73588 0	Bunny Bonanza	£3.99	❏
0 340 73589 9	Ferret Fun	£3.99	❏
0 340 73590 2	Rat Riddle	£3.99	❏
0 340 73592 9	Cat Crazy	£3.99	❏
0 340 73605 4	Pets' Party	£3.99	❏
0 340 73593 7	Foal Frolics	£3.99	❏
0 340 77861 X	Piglet Pranks	£3.99	❏
0 340 77878 4	Spaniel Surprise	£3.99	❏
0 340 85204 6	Horse Hero	£3.99	❏
0 340 85205 4	Calf Capers	£3.99	❏
0 340 85206 2	Puppy Prizes	£3.99	❏

All Hodder Children's books are available at your local bookshop, or can be ordered direct from the publisher. Just tick the titles you would like and complete the details below. Prices and availability are subject to change without prior notice.

Please enclose a cheque or postal order made payable to *Bookpoint Ltd*, and send to: Hodder Children's Books, 39 Milton Park, Abingdon, OXON OX14 4TD, UK. Email Address: orders@bookpoint.co.uk

If you would prefer to pay by credit card, our call centre team would be delighted to take your order by telephone. Our direct line *01235 400414* (lines open 9.00 am–6.00 pm Monday to Saturday, 24 hour message answering service). Alternatively you can send a fax on *01235 400454*.

TITLE		FIRST NAME		SURNAME	

ADDRESS	

DAYTIME TEL:		POST CODE	

If you would prefer to pay by credit card, please complete:
Please debit my Visa/Access/Diner's Card/American Express (delete as applicable) card no:

Signature .... Expiry Date: ....

If you would NOT like to receive further information on our products please tick the box. ❏